#6

Karen's
Little Sister

**Here are some other books
about Karen
that you might enjoy:**

Karen's Witch

Karen's Roller Skates

Karen's Worst Day

Karen's School Picture

Karen's
Little Sister

ANN M. MARTIN

Illustrations by Susan Tang

A
LITTLE
APPLE
PAPERBACK

SCHOLASTIC INC.

New York   Toronto   London   Auckland   Sydney
Mexico City   New Delhi   Hong Kong   Buenos Aires

No part of this publication may be reproduced in whole or in part,
or stored in a retrieval system, or transmitted in any form or by any means,
electronic, mechanical, photocopying, recording, or otherwise,
without written permission of the publisher. For information
regarding permission, write to Scholastic Inc., Attention:
Permissions Department, 555 Broadway, New York, NY 10012.

ISBN 0-439-37965-2

Copyright © 1989 by Ann M. Martin.
All rights reserved. Published by Scholastic Inc.
THE BABY-SITTERS LITTLE SISTER and
LITTLE APPLE PAPERBACKS are trademarks
and/or registered trademarks of Scholastic Inc.

12 11 10 9 8 7 6 5 4 3 2 1   2 3 4 5 6 7/0

Printed in the U.S.A.   40

First printing of this revised edition, February 2002

This book is for
Ann and David,
Laura and Johnny,
Shortie the dachshund,
and, of course,
Blaze Midnight the rat.

Rocky and Midgie

Hello. Here I am again. It's me, Karen Brewer. I am six, going on seven, years old. I have some freckles and a little brother who is four. I wear glasses. Once I broke my wrist. I had to wear a cast.

Do you want to know the most interesting thing of all about me? I have *two* families. That's because a long time ago, my mommy and daddy got divorced. Then they each got married again. Mommy married Seth. He is my stepfather. Daddy married Elizabeth. She is my stepmother. Most of the

1

time, my brother Andrew and I live with Mommy and Seth.

Mommy and Seth live in a little house. Seth has a dog and a cat. The dog's name is Midgie. The cat's name is Rocky. I like Seth because he likes animals and children.

Daddy and Elizabeth live in a big house. That is a good thing because an awful lot of other people live there with them. To begin with, Elizabeth has four children. They are Sam and Charlie, who are in high school, and Kristy, who is thirteen. She is one of my favorite people in the world. The last one is David Michael. He is seven. He is a pain and a bother. Sam, Charlie, and David Michael are my stepbrothers. Kristy is my stepsister. Another person at the big house is Nannie. Nannie is Elizabeth's mother, so she is sort of my grandmother.

Then there is Emily Michelle. Daddy and Elizabeth adopted her. She came from a faraway country called Vietnam. Emily is two. She is my adopted sister. Mostly, I think of her as my little sister.

I have special names for Andrew and me. I call us Karen and Andrew Two-Two. I got the names from the title of a book my teacher once read to us. It was called *Jacob Two-Two Meets the Hooded Fang*.

Andrew and I are two-twos because we have two of almost everything. We have two families. We have two houses. (Andrew and I live at the big house every other weekend.) I have two stuffed cats, one at each house. I have two bikes, one at each house. Andrew and I have clothes and toys at each house. We also have two dogs and two cats — Rocky and Midgie are at the little house, and at the big house are Shannon the puppy and Boo-Boo, Daddy's fat old cat.

You know what I wish, though? I wish I had a pet of my own. Rocky and Midgie and Shannon and Boo-Boo belong mostly to other people. Rocky and Midgie are Seth's, Shannon is David Michael's, and Boo-Boo is Daddy's. Sometimes I pretend they are mine, though.

3

One night, Rocky and Midgie were in my room at the little house. We were playing a game. I had closed the door to keep them in.

I was the mother. Rocky and Midgie were my children.

"Come here, Rocky," I said. "It's time for you to get dressed."

I pulled Rocky into my lap. I tied a doll's bonnet on his head. This was not easy. "Mrow!" said Rocky.

"Hold still," I told him. "I have to put your — Midgie, get back in bed!" Midgie was supposed to be napping in my doll's bed.

He jumped out.

Rocky pawed at his bonnet until it came off.

Then they both ran to the door.

"Oh, *darn!*" I cried.

"Karen, what's going on in there?" called Mommy.

"Nothing," I answered.

I opened my door. Rocky and Midgie flew into the hall. They darted down the stairs.

"I wish," I said out loud, "that I had a pet of my *own.*"

Emily Michelle

"Karen! Andrew! Are you ready to go to Daddy's?" asked Mommy.

It was a special Friday evening. It was a going-to-Daddy's Friday.

Andrew and I ran to Mommy in the kitchen. Our knapsacks were packed. One nice thing about being a two-two is that you hardly have to remember to take anything with you when you go from one house to the other. Just a few things that fit into a knapsack.

"We're all set!" I said.

Mommy had put her coat on. Her car keys were in one hand. Her pocketbook was in the other.

Mommy and I look alike. We both have blond hair and freckles and wear glasses. Andrew looks a little like us. He has blond hair, too, but not as many freckles, and no glasses.

"Let's go!" said Andrew.

Mommy drove us to the big house. "Goodbye!" she called as Daddy let us in the front door. "Have fun! See you on Sunday! I love you!"

"Love you, too!" said Andrew and I.

And suddenly we were in the big house. We were surrounded by people and noise and excitement.

"Hi, Professor," David Michael said to me.

That's what he started calling me when I got glasses. It is not a mean nickname. It is a nice one.

Daddy walked into the hallway carrying Emily. Emily was fussing and crying and rubbing one of her ears. She does that a lot. It is a pain.

"What's wrong with Emily?" I asked.

"Yeah. Why is she crying?" asked Andrew.

"We don't think she's feeling too well," Daddy answered. "We think she might have another earache."

Daddy leaned over and kissed Andrew and me. He couldn't hug us, though, because his arms were full of Emily. Daddy always used to hug us when we came for the weekend.

Emily didn't stop crying. She cried while the rest of us kids ate supper. Daddy and Elizabeth and Nannie had been invited to a dinner party, but now they could not decide whether to go. Daddy kept feeling Emily's forehead and saying, "I think she has a fever. Maybe we shouldn't leave."

Finally Elizabeth took Emily's temperature. No fever.

Nobody paid a speck of attention to Andrew and me. I was gigundo mad. We don't

see the big-house people very often. It wasn't fair that Emily got all the attention.

I looked at Andrew. He looked at me. We were not happy. Andrew used to be the youngest at the big house. I used to be the youngest girl. Now Emily is the baby. She has ruined everything.

Anyway, Daddy and Elizabeth and Nannie finally went to their dinner party. Charlie and Sam went to a basketball game at their school. Kristy was left baby-sitting.

Usually, I love having Kristy for my sitter. She is a good sitter. She and her friends even started a group called the Baby-sitters Club. But that night was no fun. Emily fussed and fussed. Kristy rocked her and read to her and spent an hour trying to get her to go to sleep.

She did not even have time to read me a bedtime story.

I decided that I did not like having a little sister.

The Grumpy Morning

When I woke up the next morning, I was cranky. I was in a bad mood. I felt grumpy all over.

"I hope Emily behaves herself today," I said crossly to Moosie. Moosie is my stuffed cat. I always sleep with him and with Tickly, which is half of my special blue blanket. (The other half is at Mommy's.) "If Emily does not behave herself, maybe I will just go back to Mommy's. At Mommy's, I don't have a little sister."

I had not slept well the night before. Who

can sleep with so much noise? All night, at least once every hour, Emily had woken up and cried. Then some adult had had to wake up, too, and go into her room and rock her or sing to her or give her some milk.

I decided that if anyone said to me, "Goodness, you're grumpy today, Karen," I would answer, "That is because I could not sleep last night, thanks to Emily. She made too much noise."

I rolled out of bed and got dressed. Sometimes I like to wear skirts, even on Saturdays. So I put on a blue-jean skirt and a pink-and-white-striped top. Then I pulled on pink socks and my white sneakers.

I brushed my hair.

I made my bed.

I put Moosie and Tickly on top of my bed.

I thought about Goosie (my other stuffed cat) and the other half of Tickly over at Mommy's house. Maybe I would be sleeping with *them* that night.

Finally I went downstairs. In the kitchen

I found Daddy, Elizabeth, Nannie, Kristy, and Emily. All the boys were still asleep.

Emily was in her high chair and she was fussing. As usual.

Nannie put her hand on Emily's forehead and said, "Now I think she does have a fever."

Elizabeth said, "I think she should definitely go to the doctor. Her ear is still bothering her. I'm sure she has another ear infection."

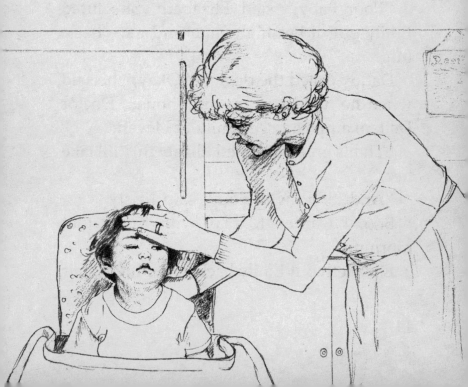

Daddy said, "I'll call the doctor right now."

No one noticed me, so finally I said in a gigundo loud voice, "GOOD MORNING!"

Emily cried harder.

Daddy said, "Karen, keep your voice down, please. Emily isn't feeling well."

I sat down at the table in a huff.

I crossed my arms and stared at Emily Michelle. Be quiet, be quiet, be quiet, I thought. But Emily would not stop crying.

"Poor baby," said Elizabeth. She lifted Emily out of her high chair and gave her a hug.

Daddy called the doctor. "Okay," he said when he had hung up the phone. "Doctor Dellenkamp can see Emily at eleven."

"That's great," replied Elizabeth. "I'll take her."

"And I'll go with you," said Kristy.

Boo. I wanted to play with Kristy that morning.

Elizabeth put Emily back in her high chair

and gave her a bowl of Krispy Krunchy cereal.

"May I have some Krispy Krunchies, too, please?" I asked.

"Oh, Karen, I'm sorry," said Elizabeth. "I didn't know you wanted any. I gave Emily the last of the box."

Double boo. I stuck my tongue out at Emily.

Just then, Emily knocked over her bowl of cereal. The milk splashed on my blouse.

"Emily!" I cried. "Bad girl!"

Emily burst into tears.

Daddy scolded me.

I could not wait for Emily to leave for her doctor's visit.

Shannon, Boo-Boo, and Pat the Cat

It was not a good day.

Emily was ruining the weekend.

When the clock said twenty to eleven, I breathed a huge sigh of relief. That was because Elizabeth, Emily, and Kristy left the house then. They were on their way to Dr. Dellenkamp's.

I didn't understand one thing, though. Why did Kristy have to go? She gets to see Emily every day. She *lives* with her. But she only gets to see me two weekends out of every month. What was so special about

Emily and her ear? She was always getting earaches.

I waved sadly to Kristy as Elizabeth drove down the street.

Then I sat on our front steps. It was nice and peaceful without Emily and her squawking and crying. But I wanted to do something. I walked around to our back-yard. I found David Michael, Andrew, Shannon, and Boo-Boo there.

Goody! I thought. I can play with one of the pets.

Shannon was busy chasing sticks that the boys were throwing, so I would have to play with Boo-Boo. Boo-Boo was in Daddy's herb garden.

He was asleep.

"Boo-Boo," I whispered. "Boo-Boo . . . *Boo-Boo* . . . BOO-BOO!"

Boo-Boo stirred, but he did not even open an eye.

I shook him gently. "Wake up! Wake up!"

"Grrr," growled Boo-Boo. That was cat talk for, "Go away and let me sleep." See?

Emily had even kept Boo-Boo awake during the night.

I left Boo-Boo alone. Who wants to play with someone who doesn't want to play with you? Boy. Now I really, really, really wished for a pet of my own.

Then I got an idea. I ran inside and called Hannie Papadakis. Hannie is my big-house best friend. She lives across the street and one house down. (I have a little-house best friend, too. Her name is Nancy Dawes and she lives next door to Mommy. Hannie and Nancy and I are in the same class at school.)

"Hannie?" I said. "Want to come over? . . . You do? Oh, good. Can you bring Pat? I promise that Boo-Boo won't bother her." Pat is Hannie's kitten. I love Pat. She is a very good kitten. She is nice, unlike other cats I can think of who won't wake up or won't wear dolls' bonnets.

So Hannie came over, carrying Pat in her arms.

We sat in my front yard.

"Hi, Pat," I said, "Hi, Pitty-Pat."

Pat purred and purred.

"What shall we play?" Hannie asked me.

I thought for a moment. "Let's play house. I'll be the mother, you be the father, and Pat will be our baby."

"Okay," said Hannie.

But Pat was frisking around the yard. She did not look like she was going to want to be our baby.

"Wait," I said. "I have a better idea. Look at those dandelions growing by our walk.

Let's make Pat some fancy dandelion jewelry."

So we did. We made her four little bracelets and a necklace.

Just as we were finishing the necklace, Elizabeth's car pulled into the drive.

"There are Kristy and Emily and Elizabeth!" I cried, jumping up. "I have to go find out what the doctor said about Emily's ear."

Emily's Ears

When I asked Elizabeth about Emily's ear, she just said, "At lunchtime I'll tell everybody what the doctor said."

It was almost lunchtime anyway, so Hannie took Pat home. Pat looked so, so lovely in her dandelion jewelry.

My brothers and Kristy and I helped make lunch. We took everything out of the refrigerator, put it on the counter, and fixed our own lunches. When we sat down to eat, the whole family was at the long kitchen table. Daddy sat at one end and Elizabeth

sat at the other. Kristy, Andrew, Nannie, and I were squeezed onto one side, and Sam, Charlie, and David Michael sat across from us. Emily was in her high chair, next to Elizabeth.

"Well," said Elizabeth, "I have an announcement to make."

Everybody stopped eating and looked at her.

"Is the announcement about Emily?" I asked.

"Yes," replied Elizabeth. "The doctor said she does have another ear infection. Then she said that Emily has had too many ear infections. She wants to put some special tubes in her ears."

"Tubes in her ears!" exclaimed David Michael.

"Yes. They will help drain fluid when she gets a cold, so that it won't infect her ears. When she's a little older, the tubes will be taken out."

"Ew," I said.

"How do they put the tubes in her ears?" asked Andrew.

"Emily will have to go into the hospital," Elizabeth replied. "Just overnight. She'll have an operation in the morning and the surgeon will put the tubes in. It's actually pretty simple. Emily can come home later that day. Doctor Dellenkamp wants to do this in two weeks, when Emily's earache has cleared up."

Oh, that is great, I thought. That is just great. Guess when two weeks would be? It would be Andrew's and my next visit to the big house. Everyone would be fussing over Emily then. Some of the adults would probably want to stay at the hospital with her. Maybe *all* of the adults would want to stay at the hospital. Maybe even *Kristy* would want to.

What a fun weekend that would be.

I put my fork down. I was mad. How come Emily got all the attention? She was going to get to stay in the hospital. I didn't even have to stay in the hospital when I broke my wrist. I just went to the emergency room for awhile.

Boo, boo, boo.

"Hey, Everybody! Look at Me!"

There was only one good thing about the rest of the weekend. That was that Emily stopped crying and rubbing her ear. Dr. Dellenkamp had given her some medicine and she started to feel better right away.

But nobody could stop talking about Emily.

On Saturday afternoon, I walked into the den. Daddy and Charlie and Emily were there. A baseball game was on TV, but Daddy and Charlie were not watching it. Daddy was holding Emily in his lap and saying, "Maybe Emily's speech will get better after the tubes are in her ears."

"What do you mean?" asked Charlie.

"Well, she doesn't talk much for a two-year-old," said Daddy. "Maybe that's because she doesn't hear well."

Nobody had noticed me yet, so I turned a somersault into the den and landed at Daddy's feet.

"Look at me!" I cried.

Daddy said, "Very nice, Karen. . . . Poor Emily. How awful to have ears full of fluid."

I left the room.

At dinner that night, Elizabeth said, "I wonder how Emily will feel when she's in the hospital. I'm worried. She'll probably be scared to death."

"Maybe one of us can spend the night with her," suggested Nannie.

I hoped it would be Nannie or Elizabeth, not Daddy.

"I was scared when I had my tonsils out," said Charlie. "Remember?"

I stood up and announced, "We learned

a new song in music class last week. Want to hear it?" Before anyone could answer, I began singing, *"You are my sunshine, my only sunshine."*

But Sam ruined it by joining in with, *"Ay, ay, ay-ay. I am the Frito Bandito. I like Fritos corn chips. I like them, I do —"*

I sang louder so my family could hear *me*, but Elizabeth said, "Quiet down, both of you. Let's have a peaceful meal."

Why did we have to quiet down? I wondered. Emily probably couldn't hear us anyway.

On Sunday, all I wanted was for someone to pay attention to me.

First, I tried being nice. I fixed Emily's breakfast for her.

Nannie said, "Oh, look how well Emily is eating. She must be feeling better."

Did anyone say, "Thank you, Karen"? No. They did not.

Then I tried being naughty. At lunchtime, I put some peas in my spoon. I boinged them across the table. They landed on the tray of Emily's high chair.

"Oh, what a mess," said Elizabeth. "Don't worry, Emily. I'll clean it up for you."

Later that afternoon, I waited until the food had settled in my stomach. Then I ran into the living room, where Daddy, Elizabeth, and Nannie were sitting. For once, Emily was not with them.

"Hey, everybody! Look at me!" I cried. I did a handstand, but I fell over.

"Karen," said Daddy, "is your knapsack packed? You and Andrew need to be ready to leave when Mommy comes."

I sat up slowly.

"It's packed," I said grumpily.

Then I stalked out of the living room.

I could not wait to go back to the little house.

A Pet for Karen

When Andrew and I were back at the little house that night, I felt sad.

I sat on my bed for awhile and just looked at Goosie. I did not even talk to him.

Then I sat on a chair in our den. I swung my feet back and forth. I did not turn on the TV.

Andrew came into the den and said, "Can I watch *Captain Tornado?*" He knows I hate *Captain Tornado.*

"I don't care," I answered.

I wished Midgie would push his wet nose into my hand, or that Rocky would curl up in my lap. But Rocky and Midgie were fast asleep on the rug in the laundry room.

When Andrew turned on *Captain Tornado* I went back up to my bedroom. After awhile, Mommy and Seth came in. They sat down next to me.

"Karen," said Mommy, "I don't think you had a very happy weekend at Daddy's. Is that right?"

I nodded.

"Do you want to tell us about it?" asked Seth.

"All anyone talks about over there is Emily. Emily this. Emily that. Emily, Emily, Emily. Sometimes I was lonely this weekend."

"You know Daddy still loves you, though, don't you?" asked Mommy. "And Elizabeth and Kristy and your brothers and everyone love you, too."

"I guess," I replied. "But I didn't feel like they loved me."

Seth put his arm around me. Mommy kissed my cheek.

"You know what I wish?" I said.

"What?" asked Mommy and Seth.

"I wish I had a pet of my own. I wish I had something that belonged to me, something I could take care of that would love *me* as much as I loved it. Hannie has Pat, and David Michael has Shannon."

Mommy and Seth looked at each other. They raised their eyebrows.

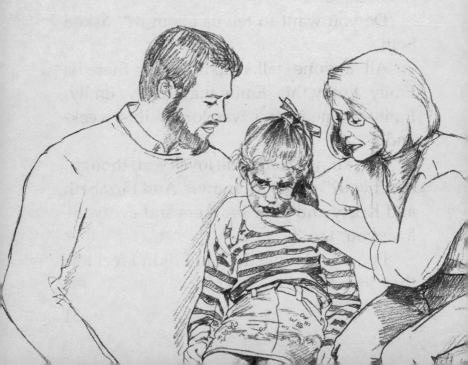

"Well," said Mommy after a moment, "I guess you are old enough to have a pet."

"*Really?!*" I cried.

"Really," Mommy answered. "*If* you promise to take care of your pet yourself — except for when you're at Daddy's. Then Seth and I will be happy to take care of it for you."

"Oh! Oh, goody, goody, goody! I can't believe it!" I exclaimed. Then I remembered to add, "Thank you. I promise to care for my pet. I'll never forget."

"Just one thing," spoke up Seth. "You'll have to get a small pet. No more dogs or cats. We already have Rocky and Midgie. Another dog or cat would be too much trouble. But you may choose whatever kind of small pet you want."

"Can I have a pet, too?" asked a voice from the doorway. It was Andrew. He looked pleadingly at Mommy and Seth.

"When you are six," Mommy told him gently.

I was feeling so happy that I said to my

brother, "Andrew, you can share my pet sometimes, okay?"

"Okay!"

Mommy and Seth and Andrew left me alone then. I began to think. What kind of pet did I want? A hamster or a gerbil? No, they're too small. A rabbit? Maybe. A snake? Nah. Too yucky. Fish? No, they aren't any fun. A frog? Not very cuddly. Too bad about no more cats and dogs. What I wanted was a cat of my own like Pat. But at least I was going to get a pet.

When I fell asleep that night I dreamed of animals.

The Baby Bird

On Monday afternoon after school, I was still thinking about pets. I put my jacket on and wandered around the backyard. I sat down on a rock.

What kind of pet? What kind of pet? I wondered. A mouse? No, *much* too small. A turtle? No, even less cuddly than a frog, although it would be fun to watch a turtle hide in its shell. A guinea pig? Maybe. But if I were going to get a guinea pig, I might as well get a rabbit. In kindergarten, our class pet was a rabbit named Nibbles, and I liked Nibbles very much.

A smart animal would be fun. I could teach it tricks or — Hey! I thought. What about a parrot? I could teach it to *talk*. That would really be great!

I stood up and began walking around, thinking. I could teach a parrot to say, "Hello, Karen," or even to sing "You Are My Sunshine." We could sing together. We could perform. Karen Brewer and her singing parrot. We would be famous.

I was thinking so hard about being famous that I wasn't watching where I was going. I nearly stepped on something in the grass. The something was alive.

"Yikes!" I cried.

I jumped back.

Then I bent down to see what it was.

It was a baby bird. It was flopping around, looking scared. I didn't think it was hurt, but it seemed awfully small. Maybe it had fallen out of its nest. That happens sometimes.

Where was the bird's mother? I wondered. Then I remembered something that Ms. Colman had told our second-grade class. Ms. Colman is our teacher, and she is very, very smart. Nice, too. Ms. Colman had said that if a mother or father animal smells the scent of a human on its baby, it will abandon the baby. It will leave the baby forever.

I did not want that to happen to this baby, so I backed away. I sat down on the rock again and watched the bird. I waited for its mother or father to come swooping out of the sky and rescue it.

No big bird came.

But Rocky appeared. I saw him amble around the corner of the house. Uh-oh! I would have to rescue the bird myself. I ran into the kitchen to get a pair of oven mitts. I hoped I could get back to the bird before Rocky saw him.

Luckily I did. Rocky was sitting by the porch. I dashed past him and scooped the bird up in the mitts. The bird squawked wildly. It flapped its tiny wings. But I managed to carry it inside.

"Mommy!" I cried. "Andrew! Come see what I found!"

Mommy and Andrew ran into the kitchen.

"What is it?" asked Mommy.

"A baby bird. I found it in the grass. I think it fell out of its nest. I was waiting for its mother to get it, but then Rocky came into the yard. I had to rescue it. What should we do with it?"

"For now," said Mommy, "let's just make it comfortable. We'll fix it up in a shoe box. Then we'll wait for Seth to come home from work. He'll know what to do. Seth is good with animals."

So Andrew and I put some soft rags and a cup of water in the shoe box. We put the bird on the rags. Then we waited for Seth.

A Big Job

Seth did not come home for two more hours. The bird squawked and flapped in the little box. It did not look very happy.

Squawk, squawk, squawk.

Flap, flap, flap.

I felt bad for the bird. It looked the way I felt when I did not want to go to the dentist. Or when I was scared or mad.

"Quiet down, birdie," I said.

The bird would not be quiet.

I started to feel annoyed. I wanted to help the bird, but I did not know how.

"Mommy?" I asked. "May I pat the bird?"

"I suppose so," Mommy answered. "Be very gentle."

I stroked the bird's feathers. "It's all right," I told the bird. "You'll feel better soon."

I was gigundo happy when Seth finally came home.

"Seth! Seth! Look what I found in the yard!" I held the box toward him. "What should we do? Mommy said you would know."

"Well," Seth replied slowly, "we can take care of the bird, but it will be a big job. Are you ready to help with a big job?"

"I'm ready," I said, feeling important.

"It's a good thing the bird is not hurt," said Seth. "It's just a little young. Still, it will need lots of care. All the care its mother would have given it."

Seth got busy collecting things — an eyedropper, some water, some grass and leaves and rags, and more.

"Do you think the bird is a boy or a girl?" I asked Seth.

Seth scratched his head. "I don't know," he replied.

"Well, I think it's a boy," I said, "so we can start calling the bird a 'him.' "

Seth grinned. Then he made a nest for the bird out of the grass and leaves and rags. Next he showed me the special food that he had fixed for the bird. He sucked it into the eyedropper.

"Now, Karen," he said, "baby birds eat very often. We will have to feed your bird every two hours or so. All day and all night for awhile. Just like this."

Seth showed me how to feed the bird with the eyedropper. Right away, the bird seemed happier. It settled down. It stopped squawking so much. I thought of Emily. She had stopped crying after Dr. Dellenkamp had given her the medicine for her ear. Emily and the bird were sort of alike. They needed big people to help them with some things.

I was glad my bird felt better.

"Karen?" said Mommy. "Do you think

you can remember to feed the bird every two hours after school? Seth and I will help you at night and while you're at school, but the rest of the time, he is your responsibility."

I nodded. "I can do it. I want to help the bird grow up. By the way, you don't have to get me a pet now. The bird will be my pet. You know why? I had just decided that the pet I would ask for was a parrot. And

then I almost stepped on the bird. So the bird will be my pet instead. Okay?"

Mommy and Seth glanced at each other. They did not say anything.

But, "Squawk!" went the bird.

"Oh, you are so cute, little birdie," I said, "I will have to name you. Then I can call you something besides 'him' and 'birdie.' "

I looked happily into the bird's box. At last I had a pet of my own.

Magic Tastee

Not long after the bird's first feeding, Seth said, "Oh, I just remembered! Baby birds are used to warm nests. Their mothers keep the nests warm. So do their brothers and sisters. This little guy must be getting chilly. We'll have to warm him up."

Seth turned on the oven and opened the door.

"You're going to cook the birdie?" shrieked Andrew.

"Oh, no, honey. Of course not," Mommy answered in a rush.

Seth looked around at us. I could tell he was trying not to smile.

"No way," he replied. "I'm just going to heat the nest for him."

"Oh." Andrew let out a huge sigh of relief.

Seth gently took the bird out of the nest and set him on a rag in the box. Then he stuck the nest in the oven. He left it there for ten minutes. Then he put it back in the bird's box.

I touched it carefully. It wasn't too hot. Just nice and warm.

Seth put the bird in the nest. Right away, the bird fell asleep. I guess he needed naps like Emily.

"Thank you, Seth," I said.

"You're welcome," he replied. "But remember. Our work has just begun."

Why do grown-ups make everything seem like a chore? I wondered. I didn't mind feeding my bird and warming his nest.

A little while later, the bird woke up. He began to squawk again.

"Feeding time!" announced Seth, even though we were in the middle of our own dinner.

"Okay," I said. I stood up from the kitchen table. I found the eyedropper and filled it with food. Then I sat on the floor next to the bird's box and fed him the way Seth had shown me.

The bird grew quiet. I stroked his soft feathers. I felt just like his mother. I was feeding him and taking care of him and making him happy.

When the eyedropper was empty, the bird hopped into his nest and went to sleep again.

"Now I will have to name the bird," I told Mommy and Seth and Andrew. We were cleaning up the kitchen. "He needs a really good name. I am going to go to my room to think. And I will take the bird with me. That way, I can close my door and Rocky will not be able to get him."

So I carried the bird and the box and the eyedropper and the food upstairs. I set the box at the foot of my bed. I closed my door. Then I knelt by the box.

"What should I name you?" I asked the bird. (He was still asleep.) "I think I should name you after something I like."

I made a list of things I like:

Magic tricks
Roller-skating
Cats
Dogs
All animals
Mr. Tastee, the ice-cream man
Andrew and Kristy and
my families

I looked at the list. I couldn't name the bird Roller Skates. I couldn't name him Cat or Dog. Then I got a great idea. I could name him after *two* things I like. I would call him Magic Tastee. That was a very, very

special name. I hoped the bird would like it.

I wrote his name on his box and set the box on the radiator so Magic Tastee could stay warm and toasty during the night.

The Best Bird
in the Whole World

All that night, whenever Magic Tastee squawked, Mommy or Seth or I would get up and feed him. He squawked six times, so each of us got up twice.

The next morning, I felt very sleepy. But I was glad to see that Magic Tastee looked fine. He hopped around in his box. He even chirped a couple of times.

"What kind of bird do you think Magic Tastee is?" I asked Seth as he drove me to school.

"I think he's a sparrow," Seth replied.

"He will probably not grow to be a very big bird."

"That's okay," I said, "because he is the best bird in the whole world. . . . Seth?"

"Yes?"

"Did you notice that I remembered to heat Magic Tastee's nest before we left? And tonight I will put it on the radiator again."

"I'm very proud of you," said Seth. He smiled at me.

"And Magic Tastee seemed much happier today. He was hopping all over."

"You are doing a good job. You're being very responsible."

Seth let me off in front of school and I ran inside. I ran straight to my classroom. A few other kids were already there. And Ms. Colman was sitting at her desk.

"Guess what! Guess what!" I shouted.

"Karen," said Ms. Colman gently. "Use your indoor voice."

"Sorry," I said. I put my things away in my cubby. Then I joined Hannie and Nancy. They were talking to Natalie Springer and

Ricky Torres in the back of the room. Natalie and Ricky wear glasses like I do.

"Guess what," I said to them in a quieter voice. "I found a bird yesterday. It was lost from its mother. So I put it in a box, and we made a nest for it and we're feeding it about every two hours, and I named it Magic Tastee!"

"Cool," said Natalie.

"Awesome," said Nancy.

"Neat," said Hannie.

"What kind of name is Magic Tastee?" asked Ricky.

I made a face at him. Ricky is a gigundo pain.

A few more kids came into the room. Nancy told them about Magic Tastee. They had lots of questions. Everyone gathered around me. I just love being in the middle of things and answering questions.

As soon as I got home that day, I ran to Magic Tastee's box. He was fluttering around, chirping happily.

"Aw, you are so cute, Magic Tastee," I told him. I stroked his feathers. "I love you. Do you know that?"

Mommy came into my room then.

"How was he today?" I asked.

"Full of beans," said Mom. "He seems to love his food."

"Well, I'll take over now," I said importantly. "Oh, Mommy, I am so glad to have a pet at last."

Mommy looked thoughtful. "One day soon he will learn to fly, Karen," she said.

But I was not listening. I was gathering up Magic Tastee's nest so I could warm it for him again.

Show and Share

I found Magic Tastee on Monday. All that week, he changed. He got a little bigger. He ate more, but he did not eat as often. He hopped around more. He chirped more and squawked less. I thought I was being a very good mommy to Magic Tastee.

On Thursday, Seth said to me, "It's time to move Magic Tastee into a bigger box. And we will have to cover it with a screen. Otherwise, Magic Tastee might escape and fly around the house. Have you noticed that he is trying to learn to fly?"

"Yes," I said, even though I had not noticed at all. I had just seen that Magic Tastee was hopping higher and fluttering more.

So Seth found a bigger box in our garage. Then he went to the hardware store. He bought a piece of screen. He made a top for Magic Tastee's new box.

Every Monday, Wednesday, and Friday, we have Show and Share time in Ms. Colman's class. You only have to tell something or bring something to show if you want to. I almost always have something for Show and Share.

Guess what I brought to school on Friday. Magic Tastee! Actually, Mommy brought him. She brought him just for Show and Share, and she took him home right afterward. I did not tell Hannie or Nancy or anyone except Ms. Colman what I was going to do.

I was very excited about my surprise.

At Show and Share time on Friday, Ms. Colman said, "Okay, boys and girls, who has something to show or share?"

Seven kids raised their hands. I was one of them.

Then Ms. Colman said, "I know what Karen has to show us, and it will be a surprise. It should be here any minute. While we wait, Ricky, why don't you share something with us?"

Ricky got up from his desk. He stood in front of the classroom. What he had to show was a dumb old tooth he had lost. The Tooth Fairy had given him a dollar for it.

Ricky was just sitting down when a knock came at our door. Ms. Colman opened it. There was Mommy carrying Magic Tastee in his box! When she walked into the room, all the kids went, "Oooh."

I stood proudly in front of the room. Mommy set Magic Tastee's box on a desk. Then she sat down in the visitor's chair.

"This," I said, "is Magic Tastee. He's a

baby sparrow. I found him on Monday, and I have been feeding him and warming his nest and — "

"I can't see!" cried Audrey. Audrey sits in the third row.

"Neither can I!" said Hannie and Nancy and a whole bunch of other kids.

"Then if you're very quiet," began Ms. Colman, "you may all come to the front of the room. Remember to tiptoe and whisper."

"And I can take the screen off of the box," I added. "It will be okay."

My friends followed Ms. Colman's directions. They crowded around Magic Tastee, but they were very quiet.

"What do you feed him?" asked Ricky Torres.

"How much does he weigh?" asked Audrey.

"Do you ever let him outdoors?" asked Natalie Springer.

"What do Rocky and Midgie think of him?" asked Hannie.

"What will you do when Magic Tastee learns to fly?" asked Ms. Colman.

I answered everyone's questions — everyone's except Ms. Colman's. Why did adults keep talking to me about Magic Tastee and flying?

I did not want to think about that.

Instead I looked at all my friends. I pretended that they were a big audience and they had come to see Karen Brewer and her World-Famous Sparrow.

I just love being the center of attention.

Someday I will be gigundo famous.

Kristy's Call

One thing I do not like about being Karen Two-Two is that I don't get to see my big-house family very often.

Kristy does not like this, either. So she said, "Let's talk on the phone sometimes when you're at your mom's house."

We usually talk once or twice a week.

One Wednesday — the Wednesday after Magic Tastee had visited school, and two days before Andrew and I were supposed to go back to the big house — the phone rang.

Ring, ring.

"I'll get it!" I shouted.

"Karen, you don't need to scream," said Mommy.

"Sorry," I apologized. I ran into the kitchen.

I picked up the phone. "Hello, this is Karen Brewer," I said. I was going to say, "Hello, this is the *famous* Karen Brewer," but Mommy was in the kitchen, too. So I didn't.

"Hi, Karen. It's me, Kristy."

"Kristy!" I cried. Mommy and I looked at each other. I remembered to keep my voice down. "Hi!" I said. "Guess what. I took Magic Tastee outside today. I mean, I took him outside in his box."

"Did he like that?" asked Kristy.

Kristy already knew about Magic Tastee, since I had talked to her twice the week before. She knew how I had found him. She knew that he was growing, and that he had a new, bigger box.

"He liked it a lot, I think," I told Kristy. "You know what? I took the screen off so he could look around, and he flapped his wings and jumped right up onto the edge of the box. Then he just perched there."

"Weren't you afraid he would fly away?" asked Kristy.

"No," I replied. " 'Course not. Why would he fly away? I am his mother. Thanks to me, he feels a *lot* better. He chirps and eats and jumps around. No more squawking."

"That's good," said Kristy. "You know who else feels better?"

"Who?"

"Emily. The medicine worked. Her ear infection is gone, and she isn't fussy any-more. Well, of course, sometimes she gets a little fussy, but not the way she was when you were here the last time. That was really bad." (I was glad to hear Kristy say that.) "On Friday she goes into the hospital. I'm sure she'll be scared, but once the tubes are in her ears, she'll *really* feel better."

"Who's going to stay at the hospital with Emily on Friday night?" I asked. I just *had* to know. *Please, please, please not Daddy.*

"My mother is," replied Kristy.

What a relief, I thought. But then I began imagining Emily in the hospital. I thought of her lying in a strange bed. I thought of all the doctors and nurses coming into her room. They would probably give her shots and look in her ears and make her take medicine. Emily wouldn't understand what was going on. I began to feel sort of sorry for her. And I felt guilty for having been so mad at her before.

"Kristy," I said, "what will Emily think when she has to stay in the hospital and have an operation?"

"I'm not sure," Kristy replied. "I'm a little worried. After all, she lived in an orphanage until she was two. Then she was taken away from the only place she'd known, and brought to a strange country and a strange family. Now we're going to take her to another strange place where some strange people are going to do things to her that will probably hurt."

"Yeah," I said slowly.

Now I really felt horrible. I had yelled at Emily and called her a bad girl when she wasn't even feeling well.

I would have to do something about that.

Get Well Soon, Emily

As soon as Kristy and I got off the phone, I went upstairs to my room. I felt like crying, but I was not sure why.

"Something is wrong," I said to Goosie. "I feel bad. Emily is a pest and she gets lots of attention. But she has to go into the hospital, where she will be scared, and where she might hurt. She will not know what's happening to her. How can I call her a pest when she will be so upset?"

Goosie wanted to say something to me, so I held him up to my ear and listened.

"What?" I said. "A card? A get-well card
for Emily? Well, maybe I *should* make her
one." I looked over at Magic Tastee, who
was hopping around in his box. "I could
draw a picture of Magic Tastee for Emily,"
I said, "couldn't I?"

I made Goosie nod his head.

"Okay, then. I better get to work."

I found some plain white paper in my
desk. Then I found some crayons and Magic
Markers and glitter and glue. I set every-

thing on the table in my room. I was ready to get to work.

First I folded a piece of paper in half. With the brown Magic Marker, I drew the outline of a bird. I left plenty of space under him so I would have room to write. Then I spread glue all over the bird and sprinkled sparkles on the glue. When I was done, I had made a green bird with a red wing and a blue beak. It was a very fancy bird.

The bird did not look anything like Magic Tastee. Even so, at the bottom of the card I wrote:

THIS IS MY BIRD. HIS NAME IS MAGIC TASTEE. MAGIC TASTEE AND I HOPE THAT YOU WILL

I stopped writing there. I opened up the card. Inside I wrote:

GET WELL SOON!

I made each letter a different color. Then I signed my name. I wrote it in *cursive:*

Love, Karen

"Here, Goosie," I said. "Look at this."

I showed Goosie the card. I made him nod his head again and say in a little cat voice, "Very pretty, Karen."

Then I remembered something. I remembered how I had felt when I came home from the hospital with my broken wrist. I had been bored. Emily would probably be bored, too. So I found a coloring book that I had only colored one page in. I would give Emily the card and the book on Saturday.

I felt a little bit better about having been so mean to Emily.

Big Sisters, Little Sisters, Middle Sisters

Two days later it was another going-to-Daddy's Friday. As Andrew and I were packing our knapsacks, I said to Mommy, "What will happen to Magic Tastee while I'm gone?"

"Seth and I will take care of him," Mommy replied. "We told you we would care for any pet you got whenever you're at Daddy's. Remember?"

I nodded. "Don't forget to change his water."

"We won't."

"Or to feed him."

"Of course not."

"And take him outside."

"Right. We will leave the top off of his cage."

"Very carefully," I told Mommy. "Don't let Rocky attack him. And don't let him get away."

"But honey, he's learning to fly," said Mommy. "He needs his freedom. We can't

keep him cooped up in a box all his life. He's a wild bird."

I thought for a long time. Finally I said, "Well, Magic Tastee won't fly away and leave me. I am his mother."

When Andrew and I got to the big house, Daddy and Elizabeth and Emily were already gone. They were at the hospital. Nannie was in charge, and Kristy and all my brothers were at home.

"This isn't too bad," I said to Andrew. We were going upstairs to unpack our knapsacks. "It's just like any night when Daddy and Elizabeth go out and Nannie or Kristy baby-sits for us."

"Yup," replied Andrew. "Except that Emily isn't here."

"I know," I said. I couldn't figure out why I felt disappointed.

After I had unpacked, I put Emily's card and coloring book on my bureau so I would remember to give them to her the next day.

At supper that night I said to Nannie, "When will Emily have her operation?"

"First thing tomorrow morning," Nannie answered. "It won't take very long. Emily will be ready to come home after lunch. In fact, anyone who wants to can go to the hospital to pick her up. You can even go to her room."

"Right up to her *room?*" said Andrew.

"Cool," said David Michael.

"Yeah," said Kristy, Sam, and Charlie.

I had a feeling we would *all* be going to the hospital the next day.

When bedtime came that night, Andrew and David Michael and I brushed our teeth together. We foamed up the toothpaste in our mouths. Then, "Unh, two, fee, pit!" I said with my full mouth.

We spat into the sink and looked at all the foam. There was quite a bit of it.

Afterward, Kristy read me a bedtime story. It was called *A Baby Sister for Frances.* "You know," said Kristy, when the story was over, "now that Emily is here, my brothers and I have two little sisters — you and Emily."

"But I am not the littlest little sister anymore," I said.

"No," Kristy replied, "but you're still my first little sister. Plus, you're something else that is very special. You're a *middle* sister, which means you're an older sister *and* a younger sister. Emily will probably never get to be a middle sister."

I thought about that. Then I said, "You know what, Kristy?"

"What?"

"I love you."

"I love you, too."

"Good night, big sister."

"Good night, middle sister."

In the Hospital

The next day was Emily Day. In the morning, Daddy drove to the hospital to stay with Emily and Elizabeth.

Before he left, Nannie said to him, "The rest of us will come at two-thirty so we can all be there when the doctor says Emily can come home."

I didn't like to admit it, but I was excited about going to the hospital. I had never been in a hospital room — not the kind where you spend the night. I wanted to see what one looked like. And I wanted to see Emily and Elizabeth — especially Emily. I wanted to make sure she wasn't too scared. And I wanted to show her that I was sorry I had called her a bad girl and gotten mad at her.

At two-fifteen, Nannie called, "Everybody into the Pink Clinker! I'm driving!"

Sam and Charlie groaned. They are embarrassed to be seen in Nannie's rattly old pink car, but I like the Pink Clinker.

I grabbed the get-well card I had made for Emily and raced outside to the car. I scrambled into the front seat. Kristy crawled in after me. Then Sam and Charlie climbed into the backseat, and Andrew and David Michael sat in the third seat, which faces backward.

We all buckled our seat belts.

"Off we go!" said Nannie.

Sam and Charlie ducked down and wouldn't sit up straight until we reached the hospital.

As we were getting out of the car I said, "The last time I was here was when I got my cast off."

"Really?" said Sam. "I thought the last time you were here was when you had that brain operation. The one that made you so weird."

"Oh, *Sam*," I said.

Nannie led us into the hospital, and in no time at all we were walking through the doorway to Emily's room. I was surprised to see Emily standing up in her crib.

"Hi, Emily!" we said.

Emily just looked at us for a few moments. Then she gave us a huge smile.

She knows us! I thought. She knows *me*. She remembers me. She likes me. I felt the way I felt when I would kneel by Magic Tastee's box and he would hop over to me.

Andrew and David Michael began exploring Emily's room. It was pretty ugly and boring except for a TV set mounted way up high in a corner. That was sort of interesting. Sam and Charlie and Kristy talked to each other, and Daddy and Elizabeth and Nannie talked to a doctor who had come into the room.

So I talked to Emily. I stood by her bed and read the get-well card to her.

"Look," I said. "This is Magic Tastee. He's my bird. He's a sparrow. Maybe you can see him sometime. Okay?"

"Da," said Emily. (We're not sure what "da" means.)

I tickled Emily's toes. She giggled.

Then Elizabeth said, "Okay, everybody. We can go home now. Let's get the show on the road."

Nannie and Elizabeth put Emily's things in a little bag. Kristy lifted Emily out of her crib. And Daddy picked *me* up and said, "Thank you for making Emily the card. That was nice of you. I am very proud of you."

I kissed Daddy on his head, right on the place where he's getting bald.

Karen's Little Sister

As soon as we got home, Elizabeth settled Emily on the couch in the den. She put her pillow there and covered her with a blanket. David Michael turned on the TV and found a cartoon show that Emily likes. Kristy gave Emily her favorite stuffed animal, a poodle named Pooh. Elizabeth gave Emily her favorite book, *Caps for Sale.* And Charlie gave her a piece of chocolate.

This was just like when I had come home from the emergency room with the cast on my arm. I had stretched out on the couch and David Michael had turned on the TV. Everyone had given me things. Charlie had even given me a candy bar.

I felt just a *teensy* bit jealous. Then I remembered that I had some things for Emily, too. I ran upstairs to my room. I got the coloring book and found a box of crayons. I took a secret surprise out of my knapsack. Then I ran back to the den.

"Here, Emily," I said. "These are for you."

Emily was rubbing her ears again. She looked like she might cry. But when I sat down next to her, she stopped rubbing her ears. She even smiled.

"Da?" she said.

"Crayon," I told her, taking a red one out of the box. "Crayon."

"Cray," Emily said.

Then I opened the coloring book. "See?" I said. "You can color all these pictures."

Emily knows what crayons are for, but she is not a very good colorer yet. She scribbled all over a picture of a kitten. Then she handed the book back to me. "Kitty," she said.

"That's right!" I exclaimed. "That *is* a kitty. Good girl, Emily! Hey, Emily, I have something else for you," I said. I took the secret something from where I'd hidden it behind a couch pillow. I opened up an envelope.

"These," I said, "are *real* pictures of Magic Tastee. See him, Emily? That's my bird."

"Bird," repeated Emily.

"Yes. Good girl!"

After I had shown Emily the photos, she began to look tired. "Everybody leave the den!" I announced. "Emily needs a nap."

I tucked the blanket around my little sister. Kristy and my brothers and I tiptoed out of the den. Emily was already falling asleep.

I felt grown-up. I liked taking care of Emily the way I took care of Magic Tastee. But I did *not* like watching Daddy and Elizabeth and Kristy and everyone spend so much time with her. Daddy bought her

a pink pig, which Emily named Piggy. Kristy spent lots of time reading books to Emily that afternoon, and Charlie gave her another piece of candy.

Still, I knew how they felt. I had given her the coloring book and crayons and card, and shown her the pictures of Magic Tastee. Also, I was glad Emily did not seem too frightened after being in the hospital. She just seemed happy to be home with us again.

And at bedtime that night, Kristy and I read together for half an hour.

Where Is Magic Tastee?

On Sunday morning, Emily was much better. She woke up early and Elizabeth dressed her and took her downstairs for breakfast in her high chair.

I could tell it was going to be a regular old day.

Except for one thing. I was beginning to worry about Magic Tastee.

It started when we were finishing breakfast and Emily suddenly called out, "Bird?"

Daddy, Elizabeth, Nannie, Sam, and I were still sitting at the table in the kitchen.

We turned and looked out the window. Sure enough, a bird was in the feeder. It was a sparrow, like Magic Tastee.

In fact, for just a moment, I thought it *was* Magic Tastee. Then I saw that the bird was bigger than my pet. But that was when the worrying started. I wondered if Mommy and Seth were being careful when they took Magic Tastee outside. Were they keeping Rocky indoors? What if they let Magic Tastee hop out of his box? Would he start to fly?

I worried so much that I wanted to call Mommy. But I didn't. I did not want Mommy to think I didn't trust her.

Instead, I just kept worrying.

Magic Tastee wouldn't leave me . . . would he? He was my special pet. I saved his life. He must know that. But what if he was gone when I returned to the little house?

All day I was nice to Emily, and all day I worried.

When Mommy and Seth finally pulled up in front of Daddy's house, I ran out to their car.

"Good-bye!" I called to my big-house family.

I did not even stop to kiss or hug anyone. I just slid into the car. "Is Magic Tastee okay?" I asked.

Andrew climbed in next to me.

"He's fine, honey," said Mommy.

"Where is he?"

"Around somewhere," said Seth. "Don't worry."

"What do you mean 'around somewhere'?"

"You'll see when we get home," Mommy answered.

As soon as our car was parked by the little house, I scrambled out, dropped my knapsack, and ran to the backyard.

There was Magic Tastee's box. I looked inside. It was empty.

"Mommy! Seth!" I called. "Magic Tastee is gone! You let him escape!"

I was about to start crying when I heard a chirp. I looked up. Magic Tastee was perched on the edge of the porch roof.

"How did he get up there?" I asked Seth. He had come running into the yard.

"He flew. He's been flying a lot this weekend. To the bird feeder, even to a tree branch. He hardly uses his box anymore."

Suddenly I knew the truth. It was awful. "Magic Tastee isn't going to be my pet anymore, is he?" I said.

Mommy had joined us in the yard. "I think he's going to stick around," she said.

"He just won't need his box. He's going to be on his own. He is wild, you know."

I nodded. I understood. Magic Tastee wouldn't leave — but he wasn't going to be my special pet, either.

Tastee Bird

Two weeks went by, and guess what? Magic Tastee *didn't* leave. He really didn't. He never used his box again, but he was always in our yard.

He perched in the branches of our trees. He ate from the bird feeder. He splashed in the bird bath. He learned how to stay away from Rocky.

I could tell him from all the other birds in the yard.

He was my bird, but he wasn't my pet.

*   *   *

The next time I was at Daddy's house, Emily did something that surprised me. One morning, she handed me the coloring book I'd given her.

"Yook," she said. (That means "Look.")

I wasn't sure what I was yooking for, but I flipped through the book anyway. Suddenly Emily stopped me.

"Bird!" she announced triumphantly.

Sure enough, she had scribbled over a picture of a bird that looked like Magic Tastee.

"You bird," she said.

"My bird?" Did Emily really remember Magic Tastee? I was surprised.

And then I got a good idea. I talked to Daddy about it. Daddy thought the good idea was a great idea.

So Daddy and Kristy and Charlie and I arranged a special surprise for Emily. The surprise would take place on Monday, the day after Andrew and I went back to the little house.

In school on Monday I was very excited. I could not wait for the afternoon. Ms. Colman had to keep saying, "Karen, pay attention."

I tried to, but it was not easy.

At last, school was over and I was at home again. I looked at my watch three million times. (Not really.) I was waiting for four-thirty.

At four-thirty on the dot, Elizabeth's station wagon stopped in front of our house. Charlie was driving it. Kristy was sitting next to him. Emily was in her car seat behind them.

When they got out of the car, I began to laugh. Emily was wearing a shirt that said, "I'm the little sister." Kristy was wearing a shirt that said, "I'm the big sister."

"There's one for you, too," she said. She handed me a shirt of my own. It read, "I'm the middle sister . . . and proud of it!"

I laughed. Then I said, "Come on, you

guys. I'll show you Magic Tastee." I took Emily by the hand. Kristy and Charlie and Emily and I walked to the back of the house.

I whistled my special whistle for Magic Tastee.

A few moments later he swooped down from somewhere. He landed on a low tree branch.

I lifted Emily up to see him.

"There he is, Emily," I said. "There's Magic Tastee. Can you say 'Magic Tastee'? Can you say 'bird'?"

Emily paused. Finally she said, "Tastee bird," and smiled.

I giggled. Little sisters can be fun . . . sometimes.

When Magic Tastee flew away, I set Emily on the ground. "Okay, put on your new shirt," said Charlie.

"Why?" I asked.

"You'll see."

I ran inside and changed into the shirt.

When I went back outdoors, Charlie was holding a camera.

"Line up, you guys," he said.

Kristy and Emily and I stood in a line.

Click! went the camera.

Now I keep a copy of the three-sisters picture on my mirror at the little house.

Emily Junior

Magic Tastee had been a wild bird for more than a month when Mommy and Seth came into my room one night. I was sitting at my desk. I was wearing my blue glasses and doing my homework.

"Karen," said Mommy, "Seth and I have been thinking."

"We've been thinking hard," said Seth. "Our brains are aching."

I laughed. "Oh, Seth!"

"We were thinking," said Mommy, "that we promised you a pet of your own, but in the end, you didn't really get one. You have Magic Tastee, but he lives outdoors and you do not get to take care of him."

"That's true," I said. "I miss feeding him and watching him hop around in his box. I miss talking to him, too."

"So," Mommy went on, "we were wondering if you would like to get another pet — a real pet — since Magic Tastee is not what you had in mind."

"Really?" I cried. I jumped up from my desk. "I can really get another pet? Oh, thank you, thank you, thank you!"

I threw my arms around Mommy. Then I gave Seth a big hug, too.

That night, when my homework was done, I sat on my bed. I held Goosie in my lap.

"What kind of pet should I get?" I asked Goosie. "I do not think I want another bird. And no hamsters or mice or gerbils or fish. And Seth said no more cats or dogs."

Goosie looked like he had an idea. I held

him up to my ear so he could whisper it to me.

"An animal from a book that I like?" I repeated. "That's a great idea! Let me see. There's Paddington, but I can't get a bear. And there's Ferdinand, but I can't get a bull. . . . Wait a minute! I just *loved* Nicodemus in *Mrs. Frisby and the Rats of NIMH.* He was a wonderful, kind, smart rat. That's it! I will get a nice rat like Nicodemus. A rat will be small, but not *too* small."

I ran downstairs. "Mommy? Seth?" I said.

They were sitting in the living room. "Yes, honey?" said Mommy.

"I know what kind of pet I want. I want a rat like Nicodemus."

Mommy and Seth looked at each other. For just a second, I thought they were going to say, "No. No rats."

Instead, Mommy said, "We'll go to the pet store tomorrow."

The man at the store was very nice. He said, "We don't have any rats right now, but we can order one. It will take a week. Will that be all right?"

"Yes," I said. "It will be fine."

I did not like waiting for a whole week. The week dragged by. But I knew that when it was over I would have a pet of my own at last.

The next Tuesday, Mommy drove Andrew and me to the pet store. There was my rat. He was waiting in a cage. We bought an aquarium for him, plus some cedar shav-

ings, a water bottle, and some special rat food.

As soon as we were home again, I fixed up my rat's cage.

"This is your house," I told him. "You have everything you need. . . . Everything except a name," I added.

I thought and thought.

At last I said, "I'm going to call you Emily Junior, after my little sister."

And so I did.

About the Author

ANN M. MARTIN lives in New York City and loves animals, especially cats. She has three cats of her own, Gussie, Woody, and Willy, and one dog, Sadie.

Other books by Ann M. Martin that you might enjoy are *Stage Fright, Me and Katie (the Pest)*, and the books in *The Baby-sitters Club* series.

Ann likes ice cream and *I Love Lucy*. And she has her own little sister, whose name is Jane.

Little Sister

Don't miss #7

KAREN'S BIRTHDAY

Being a two-two might sound like fun, and it can be. But here is one thing I do not like about being a two-two: I never get to see everybody in my *whole* family at once. I either see the little-house family or the big-house family. So what I had decided I wanted for my birthday was to invite all the people at the little house and all the people at the big house to one party. I just wanted us to be together.

That was why I didn't sound so happy when Daddy asked if I wanted to take some friends to the Happy-Time Circus. It meant that once again Daddy was planning one party and Mommy was planning another.

And that was not what I wanted.

Little Sister

by Ann M. Martin
author of The Baby-sitters Club®

More Titles... ➡